ROSCO THE RASCAL

GOES TO CAMP

Rosco the Rascal #3

By Shana Gorian

Illustrations by Ros Webb

Cover Art by Josh Addessi & Tori March

CONTENTS

1.	The Wayward Hat	1
2.	The Windsurfer	7
3.	First Time Ever	13
4.	True Darkness	18
5.	Sheriff's in Town	24
6.	Snake on the Loose	29
7.	Take the Leap	37
8.	Don't Fall for That	45
9.	Ice Cream Social	52
10.	The Shadow on the Window	58
11.	Worries	64
12.	Capture the Flag	69
13.	The Plan	77
14.	Where There's Thunder	84
15.	Better Go Investigate	96
16.	Sheriff the Spy	103
17.	No More Class Clown	107
18.	Second Chance	113
19.	Rosco Knows the Way	119
20.	You Can Do It, Boy	125

Packing List:

7 Shorts
7 T-Shirts
2 Pairs of Jeans
2 Sweatshirts
7 Pairs of Underwear
7 Pairs of Socks
2 Pairs of Pajamas
Hat or Baseball Cap
2 Pairs of Sneakers
Flip Flops
Swimsuit
Beach Towel
Soap
Washcloth
Toothbrush
Toothpaste
Towel
Laundry Bag
Flashlight
Bug Spray
Sunscreen
Sleeping bag
Pillow

CHAPTER 1
THE WAYWARD HAT

The leaves on the tall, green trees surrounding the lake at Camp Hickory Ridge blew gently in the wind. A dozen cabins stood peacefully in the woods next to the lake while their occupants were away, busy with Sunday's afternoon activities.

"Remember last year, how I almost tipped us over?" said James, standing next to his dog, Rosco, and his friend Caleb on the wooden dock. The boys patiently waited their turn for a canoe as they watched several more drift by on the lake.

Caleb nodded and laughed. "You better promise you won't stand up this year!"

James, a redheaded fifth grader with

freckles, had been coming to camp every summer since he was eight years old.

"I promise! But I didn't mean to last time!" said James. "Honest. I just forgot what I was doing!"

Rosco, James's friendly German shepherd, sat listening and eagerly taking in

the action on the lake.

Besides the half-dozen canoes on the water, several older boys and girls sailed by on windsurfers. Windsurfing, a sport that combines surfing and sailing, was a popular activity at Camp Hickory Ridge.

The steady breeze was turning the campers' afternoon lesson into an exciting ride. A few sailing rigs had capsized and were floating in place, while the young sailors bobbed about in lifejackets, enjoying a dip in the cool lake.

Other campers seemed to be holding on for dear life as they sailed across the water at top speed.

One windsurfing instructor stood in the shallows giving a lesson to a cautious first-timer. Another paddled out in a canoe to the middle of the lake to help a desperate student pull his windsurfer upright again. But most of the campers were enjoying the day.

James and Caleb watched in excitement. Each boy wore an orange life vest and held a wooden oar. Several boys from their cabin were already out on the water, paddling away in their canoes.

"Okay, Rosco. You wait for us on the dock when it's our turn for a canoe," said James. Rosco looked intently at James and panted, his tongue hanging out.

The boys' counselor, Matt, gave orders to another pair of boys climbing out of a canoe. He tied the boat's rope to the wooden dock and turned to Caleb and James. "This one's for you guys!" He motioned to them.

"Let's go!" Caleb said, heading toward the canoe. Rosco followed the two of them across the dock.

The boys stopped to listen as they heard some arguing out on the lake. It seemed to be coming from their cabinmates Josh and Jeffrey, who were sharing a canoe.

It looked as though Jeffrey had tossed Josh's hat in the water, for no apparent reason, and was laughing as the hat floated away.

"Ha ha!" Jeffrey teased. "There it goes! See you later, hat!" James and the others nearby heard him say.

The wind quickly lifted the hat and carried it several yards farther.

Out in the boat, Josh stared at his hat, floating away on the lake.

"What did you do that for? That was the only hat I brought for the whole week!" he demanded.

"No reason! Just because it's funny!" Jeffrey smirked. "And look, it floats, just like our canoe! Ha ha ha!"

Why would he do that? James thought, annoyed. That wasn't funny at all.

James glanced at his dog still next to him on the dock. Rosco's gaze was fixed firmly on the moving hat. Before James could stop him, Rosco flung himself into the water.

"Rosco, where are you going?" James called in alarm. "Come back!"

But Rosco wanted to help. He was always ready to help someone in need. As a dog of action, Rosco wasn't going to let a perfectly good hat just float away from its owner.

Rosco doggy paddled quickly toward the wayward hat. When he reached it, he seized the hat with his teeth and headed toward the canoe. Many of the kids in nearby canoes stopped their boats to watch.

"What do you think you're doing, mutt?" Jeffrey called to Rosco. "Get out of here." But Rosco kept swimming toward them.

When he reached their canoe, Rosco swam up to Josh, who gratefully scooped it out of Rosco's mouth.

"Wow! Thanks, Rosco! Good dog!"

Rosco flashed his doggy smile, treading water, but wasted no time. He turned back around and began to swim toward the shore.

"Hmmph." Jeffrey pouted.

James's heart swelled with pride over his dog. That's my boy, he thought.

CHAPTER 2
THE WINDSURFER

As James watched Rosco steadily doggy paddling back to shore, a skinny, dark-haired, thirteen-year-old boy appeared on his windsurfer. The boy was trying hard to keep his balance, holding on tightly to the boom as he stood on the board. The instructor had explained to everyone that the *boom* on a windsurfer was like the handlebars on a bicycle.

But it was much harder than riding a bike, James thought. The boy was struggling to keep his boat afloat and not run into anything.

All at once, a fierce breeze hit the sail, speeding up the boy's rig. The boy tried to

avoid any obstacles in the water, but the wind was too strong. He couldn't control the sails. He was now heading straight toward Rosco.

Swimming calmly across the lake, Rosco didn't see or hear the windsurfer at all.

The boy began to panic. "I can't stop!" he hollered. "Watch out!" But the wind carried his voice away.

James began to panic, too. He raced to the edge of the dock, desperate to warn his dog. "Watch out, Rosco! Get out of the way!"

Rosco heard James's call without a second to spare. He turned and saw the disaster heading toward him. Quickly, Rosco took a deep breath and ducked underwater.

Then, using every ounce of his strength, he paddled down deeper. If Rosco were lucky, he might not get hit by the large board gliding overhead.

"Oh, no," Caleb whispered.

As fellow campers held their breath, the boy sailed onward, unable to stop. Swallowing hard, James watched as the boy passed straight through the spot in the lake where Rosco had been swimming only a moment ago.

But no terrible sound was heard—no awful bumping noise, no screeching howl of pain from Rosco—just the board cutting cleanly through the water.

The next moment, Rosco bobbed back to

the surface, unhurt.

"He did it!" Caleb cried. "Rosco did it!" He raised a triumphant fist into the air.

"Whew!" James sighed heavily with relief.

Rosco began to swim steadily back to shore again. In a few moments, he crawled safely onto the sandy beach. All of the kids nearby cheered, except for Jeffrey. Jeffrey was pouting.

James hurried across the dock and jumped down onto the sand to greet his sopping wet dog.

"Wow! That was close. You sure gave us a scare, boy!" James said. Are you okay?" Rosco stood up and shook himself, spattering drops from his wet fur all over the place. James held out a hand to cover his face. He turned his head away. But it was no use. Rosco soaked him. "Aw, man!" He cringed, smiling.

Rosco followed James back onto the dock. Tired and wet, the dog lay down in the warm sun.

"Take a rest, boy," James said. You deserve it." James turned back to Caleb, who had climbed into their canoe and was waiting for him. "Okay, I'm ready now," said James.

He stepped carefully into the canoe and sat down. Caleb untied the rope from the post on the dock.

"I don't know why Jeffrey would play a joke that like," Caleb said. "It wasn't funny at all. It was just mean, if you ask me."

"I know. It was like he just wanted attention. He sure is lucky that Rosco didn't get hurt, though. Because he'd be in serious trouble right now if Rosco had been hit by that windsurfer."

"By the way, isn't Jeffrey new this year?" said Caleb. "I don't remember him from last year."

"Yeah. It's his first time at camp," James said. "I asked him today when he was setting up his bunk."

Matt, their counselor, motioned to

Jeffrey and Josh to bring their canoe in, frowning hard at Jeffrey.

"Well, we'd better keep an eye on Jeffrey," James said, "especially since he's in our cabin."

They lifted their oars and pushed them against the dock to move the boat out into the water. "We don't know what kinds of things he might do. This probably won't be the last little joke he plays on one of us. And I don't want him ruining our week."

CHAPTER 3
FIRST TIME EVER

Mandy McKendrick was seven years old, and it was her first time ever at summer sleepaway camp. She and her brother, James, would be here for one whole week. In that amount of time, she'd get to do a lot of fun things at camp—like swimming, hiking, playing sports, creating something in the arts and crafts center, and making new friends, just to name a few. Most importantly, at least according to her brother, she'd get to be a part of his favorite activity on Thursday night—the big game of capture the flag. Mandy couldn't wait.

Despite all the excitement of the first day, Sunday, a few small tears escaped down her

cheeks as she hugged her parents.

"What if I miss you too much?" she asked them. "What will I do? Can I come home early if I get really homesick?"

"Honey, you're going to have a wonderful week," Mom said. "You'll make lots of friends in no time, and pretty soon, you won't even notice that we're not here. Just give it a chance. You'll see. You're going to love it here. Remember how excited you've been lately? And James is here if you get lonely. Rosco, too."

After they left, Mandy dried her eyes. She set up her sleeping bag and pillow on a top bunk, and waited as more and more of her cabinmates arrived.

Mom and Dad had dropped James at his cabin first, and James had already run down to the dock with his old friend, Caleb, to go canoeing. The older kids who had been to Camp Hickory Ridge before had the option to use the lake this afternoon.

But the new kids, mainly the younger ones like Mandy, had to wait for their whole cabin group to arrive before the fun could start.

Her cabin housed twenty girls, ages seven through nine. She didn't know even *one* of them yet. As each girl walked in with her luggage, choosing a bunk and saying goodbye to her parents, Mandy grew more and more anxious. To keep herself busy, she arranged some of her things in a drawer next to the bunk bed.

Soon, eight-year-old Kimberly arrived. Kim wore a big smile as she confidently carried her suitcase, sleeping bag, and pillow into the cabin. She chose the bunk below Mandy's.

Kim was as new to summer camp as Mandy was, but she wasn't worried about missing home and was quick to say so when they overheard a girl crying as her mother attempted to leave.

"You couldn't keep me home this week if you wanted to," Kim whispered to Mandy, tossing back her pigtails as she dug through her suitcase to find her bug spray and her sunscreen. "I just hope this week doesn't fly by too fast! I've been waiting all year to come to camp!"

Kim had long, brown hair and loved dogs, just like Mandy did. It didn't take long before Kim and Mandy became friends. Mandy's worries soon vanished.

After all of the kids arrived and settled in,

the seven-to-nine year old boys and girls split into teams to play a series of funny games and relay races.

First came the Crocodile Race. On each team, the campers stood in a long, straight line, placing their hands on the person's shoulders in front of them. Then they crouched down to form a crocodile, and raced to the finish line.

But Mandy and Kim were put on different teams, so once again Mandy was without a friend.

That's okay though, Mandy thought with a little more confidence.

For the next game, Mandy partnered up with another friendly girl from her cabin named Margaret. Margaret was seven years old, just like Mandy. It was the three-legged race. Both girls tripped and fell over twice, but neither one cared—it was too much fun.

Now Mandy could say that she knew at least two people here besides her brother. Little by little, the day was getting better.

CHAPTER 4
TRUE DARKNESS

After dinner, back at the cabin, Jennifer, Mandy's head counselor, told the girls to put on sweatshirts. It would get chilly as the sun went down. "We're heading out into the woods tonight, girls! Bring your flashlights for the walk back."

"Where are we going?" Mandy said to her friends as she hiked along the trail. "And what do you think we're going to do out here?" It was evening, and the sky was growing darker. She was worried about the wild animals that might be lurking in the dark woods.

"I think we're going to have a campfire!" Kim answered from ahead of her in line.

"Look!"

She pointed to a clearing area within the trees, just a short distance ahead. Inside of it was a huge pile of firewood surrounded by a large circle of rocks. Three rows of log benches lined the edge of the area.

"Oh, that makes sense," Mandy sighed with relief. "Of course."

Soon, all 120 campers at Camp Hickory Ridge—six cabin groups of twenty kids each—filed in and took their seats on the benches. James and Caleb waved to Mandy as they sat down. They all watched as a few of the counselors turned a small spark into a roaring campfire.

In no time, the sun went down and the sky went black. But the campfire was glowing bright. The smoky smell of the embers slowly burning was wonderful. The children heard the crickets chirping and saw stars appear in the sky. Mandy felt calm.

Soon, the counselors stood up in front of the fire and asked for the campers' attention.

"It's time to sing some camp songs!" Jennifer said. The rest of the counselors clapped for her. Then Jennifer and two other counselors began together. "This is a repeat-after-me-song!" they said loudly.

"This is a repeat-after-me-song!" echoed the kids.

"I said a-boom-chick-a-boom!" sang the counselors.

"I said a-boom-chick-a-boom!" sang the campers.

The song went on for several verses in funny accents and with different rhyming words. Mandy, Kim, and Margaret loved it.

"I said a-boom-chick-a-rock-a-chick-a-rock-a-chick-a-boom!" That one's going to be stuck in my head all night after all that repeating, Mandy thought, smiling.

Next, they listened to the counselors tell stories about the history of Camp Hickory Ridge. Mandy loved that, too. James had told her some of those stories before, after his first year at camp.

Mandy, Kim, and Margaret took their turns roasting marshmallows on long sticks.

"Oh no, I burned it!" Margaret cried, pulling her marshmallow out of the flames.

"I bet they'll give you another one," Kim offered. "Do you want me to ask?"

Margaret pulled the marshmallow off of the stick and plopped it into her mouth. "Hmm. No, that's okay. I've had worse," Margaret said. They all smiled.

Suddenly Mandy noticed how dark it looked beyond the campfire.

"You guys don't think they're going to tell ghost stories, do you?" Mandy whispered.

"I sure hope not," said Margaret.

After all, it was their first night in the woods, away from civilization, and wow, it was dark out, Mandy thought. Being outside in this true darkness—without a light from even a car or a house—would take some getting used to.

When the campfire was over, all three girls were relieved that not even *one* spooky story had been told.

* * *

That night, wrapped tightly in her sleeping bag on the top bunk, Mandy thought about her first day at camp.

She really liked it here. She hadn't missed Mom and Dad too much since her first few hours without them. James might be right about this place.

Her brother had been to Camp Hickory Ridge for two summers before now. He had always promised his little sister that she'd love it once she was finally old enough to go.

So far, the counselors and the other kids she'd met were nice, and the activities were fun. Her bed was cozy and warm, even if the nights were very, very dark here.

Mandy decided she wanted to stay.

CHAPTER 5
SHERIFF'S IN TOWN

Just as he was on most of the McKendrick's trips and outings, Rosco, the family dog, had been brought along to Camp Hickory Ridge, too.

Rosco was allowed to sleep on the porch of Mandy's cabin each night. Normally, bringing a pet wouldn't be allowed. But Mr. Gray, the camp director, kept his own dog at camp all summer. Mr. Gray was a good friend of their uncle's.

When Mandy's parents, Mr. and Mrs. McKendrick, had decided to take a business trip while the kids were away at camp, the generous camp director had agreed to let the kids bring Rosco along.

He figured that it would not only help the McKendricks, but he thought it would be a good deal for *him*, too. Since his dog, Sheriff, was the only pet at camp all summer, he thought that Sheriff might welcome the company of another dog.

Rosco was two years old, and he was playful and energetic. He loved making friends with other dogs and was excited to meet Sheriff. But surprisingly, Sheriff had been anything but friendly to him.

A large, older bullmastiff, who always seemed to be wearing a tired frown, Sheriff either lazed about all day or barked at the squirrels that he heard rustling in the woods.

What Mr. Gray did not realize, was that Sheriff *liked* not sharing the place with another dog. Camp Hickory Ridge was *his* territory and his alone. He meant to keep it that way.

So Rosco wasn't sure he'd be able to live up to his end of the deal. He didn't think that the grumpy, old dog wanted company at all.

Earlier today, at the relay races, Rosco had gotten a little carried away with the fun. Running across the lawn during a tennis ball relay, he'd snatched a ball when it fell to the ground. He'd run off with it, daring the kids to chase him. But they couldn't catch him, and in the process, he'd ruined any chance they had at winning that round.

But it was all in good fun. Even the kids had laughed. Rosco knew he wasn't supposed to do things like that, but he loved to play games like keep-away. Sometimes his rascally side got the better of him.

But Sheriff had not found his behavior at all amusing—not even a little bit. He'd thought Rosco was misbehaving and acting like a bratty puppy. He didn't see why the kids were laughing, and he didn't like that they were.

Earlier tonight, when Rosco trotted up to the dining hall porch for dinner, he saw two dog bowls that had been set for them outside the door. Both bowls were empty. Sheriff had gotten there first, and was already licking his chops, finishing up his meal. Rosco shot a questioning glance at Sheriff as the old grouch wandered off.

What's going on here? Rosco thought. Sheriff ate my dinner? After Sheriff ate his *own* dinner?

Sheriff turned and stared at him with cold, tired eyes and whined quietly. *Yep.*

Rosco had gotten the message, loud and clear—Rosco wasn't wanted here, not by that old grump.

Yes, Rosco was exactly right. Sheriff intended to see that Rosco had a terrible week. If he succeeded, then Rosco might never want to come back. And Sheriff would get to keep his territory all to himself.

So Rosco knew it was going to be a busy week. He had a lot to do—keep Mandy from missing home, find a way to make Sheriff warm up to him, and arrive early to every mealtime so that the crabby old dog didn't eat his food!

CHAPTER 6
SNAKE ON
THE LOOSE

On Monday, James and his cabinmates spent the morning learning to tie fishing knots and then playing flag football.

Then it was time for lunch—hot dogs, baked beans, watermelon, and bug juice. The juice didn't really have any bugs in it. It was just what Matt and Jennifer and the other counselors called any juice that was served at camp, to add a touch of the outdoors and fun to their daily meals.

Everyone joked that there *were* real bugs in it though, especially when they wanted to trick the new kids every year.

At each meal, the kids and the counselors

walked through a cafeteria line and filled their trays with delicious food, then sat together at long tables in groups of ten. Each camper and counselor was responsible for bussing his or her own tray.

After lunch, it would be time for rest hour—an hour everyday that campers spent relaxing at the cabins, resting up for more activity. Some kids even napped.

Caleb, Josh, and several others of the twenty members of their cabin left the dining hall first and reached their cabin in the woods. They began kicking off their shoes and settling in on their bunks.

James and several others from their cabin walked slowly along the wide trail, in no hurry to lie down and rest. Rest hour was their least favorite part of the day.

All of a sudden a loud holler came from the cabin.

"What was that?" James glanced at his friends in alarm. The pack of boys quickly broke into a run.

They raced inside the cabin, letting the screen door slam shut behind them.

Matt and the other two male counselors from their group hadn't yet returned from lunch.

"Snake! There's a snake!" Josh yelled.

"Where?" James cried, looking around.

"On my bed! Under the covers!" Tim answered from the corner of the room. He pointed at his bunk.

The boys rushed over. "What kind it is? Is it poisonous?" James asked.

"I don't know! I can't see the head. It just looks big and brown, with patterned lines on its back!" Tim said.

The long, thick snake had spread itself out in an S shape inside Tim's sleeping bag. Its body bulged under the covers. Its tail end stuck out.

Mike, a cabinmate who usually sat at James's table for meals, stepped closer to inspect the creature. "My brother has a pet boa at home. I can handle this," he said. He started to reach for the sleeping bag.

"Wait!" said James. "It might bite! We're not sure if it's poisonous yet!"

"I think you mean venomous. But it doesn't have a rattle—it can't be a rattlesnake," Mike said.

"I know, but still!" James answered. He brought his voice down to almost a whisper. "You can never be too careful. Can someone go grab a stick?"

One of the boys quickly rushed outside and grabbed the first long stick he could find. He brought it in and handed it to James, who handed it to Mike.

"Okay, go ahead Mike," said James.

The two of them stepped cautiously toward the bed. The rest of the large group of boys gathered around.

"Stay back, guys," James said. "Just in

case it strikes."

Mike carefully used the stick to lift up the top layer of the sleeping bag. The sleeping bag wasn't zippered so he was able to pull it back, very slowly.

Everyone waited and watched, eyes wide. Half of the snake's body, from the tail to the middle, was now visible. But nothing happened.

Surprised, James and Mike stepped a little bit closer. Using the stick, Mike swung the rest of the sleeping bag off of the beast in one fast, sweeping motion.

There it was, the whole snake! Almost three feet long and two inches thick, its devilish eyes stared straight at the boys. Its long, skinny tongue stuck out at them. But still, it didn't move—no hiss, no slither, and no strike.

"Wait! Wait a second! That isn't real; I think it's a fake!" Mike yelled. The boys all looked at each other in shock. Mike cautiously waved his hand in front of the snake's face. Nothing happened. Tim stepped closer and yanked on his sleeping bag. Still, nothing happened.

"It *is* fake!" Caleb said. The boys looked around at each other to see who had played such a rotten joke.

"Gotcha!" Jeffrey broke into laughter. "You dummies! You guys all thought it was real! Ha ha ha! You should've seen the looks on your faces! Scaredy cats!"

But no one else laughed.

"That wasn't funny, Jeffrey!" James said. "It could've easily been a real snake! We're way out in the woods! It could've slithered in while we were at lunch."

"Aw, come on. Don't you have a sense of humor? Come on, guys! It was only a joke," Jeffrey said. He glanced across the room. Everyone looked annoyed by his little trick.

Jeffrey walked over to the bed and picked up the large, rubber snake. He shoved it in Mike's face. "It's just a joke! See! Not real! Can't you guys take a joke?"

Mike grabbed the snake's hollow head and scrunched it hard with his fist. "Very funny," he said flatly.

James climbed to the top bunk and settled down on his mattress. "We should've known it was you, Jeffrey. First the hat, now this. We'd all better watch our backs with you around."

Jeffrey sat down on his own bunk. "Bunch of babies," he mumbled.

CHAPTER 7
TAKE THE LEAP

Mandy was enjoying camp. She had spent part of Monday morning in the arts and crafts room, painting a pet rock as a present for Dad. She painted hers to look like an owl, then glued on googly eyes when the paint was dry. It would be a paperweight for his desk.

She hadn't been missing home too much. But as she painted that rock, she began to wonder what her parents were doing at that very moment. Suddenly, she'd felt a little twinge of sadness.

So today during rest hour, she had taken out the notepaper that Mom had packed for her, and written her parents a short letter. She had given it to her counselor to mail.

Somehow, it felt as though her good mood had been magically restored. Writing that letter reminded her just how much fun she was having and how quickly time was passing here.

After rest hour, Mandy's cabin group went swimming. It was hot out, the perfect day for a dip in the pool.

The camp pool had a diving board that was six feet off the ground and a deep end that was twelve feet deep.

It had only been five minutes since they'd arrived at the pool, and some of the girls were already dancing about in the wide shallow end, showing off their best underwater flips and handstands. Others took a deep breath and held their noses as they ducked down under the surface, then jumped back up, straight out of the water as high as they could go. Still other girls lined up for the diving board.

"James!" Mandy cried, waving from the middle of the shallow end. She was excited to see her brother's cabin group now entering the pool gate, too. She had only seen him at the dining hall and at the all-camp activities, like the campfire last night.

James waved sweetly to his younger sister as he walked in with his friends. He held up one thumb to her with a questioning look. Then he turned it thumbs-down with a look of concern. She answered this sign language of theirs with her own thumbs-up, as if to say, "Yep, everything's fine!"

James smiled, satisfied with her answer, and followed the other boys to a wooden bench. They set down their towels and began to apply their sunscreen.

The older boys wasted no time as they cannonballed or jumped into the cool, blue water, making giant splashes that sprayed the younger girls.

Rosco was at the pool, too. He lounged in the shade of a large maple tree that stood beside the gated swimming area, enjoying the lively atmosphere in between naps. Every now and then, tiny drops of cool water splashed his warm fur. Sheriff slept at the far end of the pool yard, as far away from Rosco as he could get.

A lifeguard blew her whistle. "No running on the pavement!" she called to a boy.

Three young girls from Mandy's cabin, Izzy, Natasha, and Madison, stood at the back of the diving board line, waiting their turns to climb the ladder and use the diving board. Jeffrey walked over, stepping into place behind them.

"It's almost your turn, Izzy. Are you sure you're ready to jump from that high?" Natasha asked.

"Yes, I'm sure," Izzy said. "At least I think so." But she looked worried.

Jeffrey listened, rolling his eyes.

All of them continued to wait in line while watching the kids ahead of them take their turns.

Some of the kids seemed to be experts at using the diving board. One boy walked to the edge of the board, hopped up and down to get the board moving, and sprang up into the air. He did a somersault and landed in the pool with a giant splash.

"Oooo!" cried a group of kids who had been watching.

Soon, the three girls reached the front of the line. Natasha climbed the ladder, walked confidently to the end of the board, bounced up and down as hard as she could, jumped off the board, and grabbed her knees in the air. She landed in the water with an enormous splash.

Madison climbed the ladder, walked a bit more slowly to the end of the board, then cautiously looked to the left and to the right. She squeezed her nose between her finger and thumb, and simply stepped off the board. She hit the water with hardly a splash.

Then seven-year-old Izzy timidly climbed the ladder and began to walk stiffly across the diving board. Reaching the end, she stopped and peered over the edge. The

water looked so far down and so deep! She wasn't ready to take the leap.

But Jeffrey was still waiting at the bottom of the ladder for his turn. "Come on, kid! Just jump!" he hollered impatiently.

By this time, Natasha and Madison had climbed out of the pool and were standing beside it below, anxiously waiting for their friend. "Come on, Izzy. You can do it," Natasha chanted.

But she just couldn't jump. Izzy was scared. In fact, she was panicking. Her legs wouldn't move—not forward, not backward, not to jump, not to walk back and climb down the ladder. She began to cry.

"Come on, kid! You're holding up the line!" Jeffrey called roughly. Then he climbed a few steps up the ladder, hunching down so the counselors wouldn't notice him. "Hurry up!" But Izzy didn't move.

"Come on!" he said again. Losing his patience, he climbed to the top of the ladder and bounced up and down a couple of times. This made the board vibrate in little waves of motion. He didn't care who saw him now.

Just get it over with, kid. Just get off the board. There are people waiting, Jeffrey thought with irritation.

Izzy turned to see who had been yelling at her. The older boy at the other end of the diving board sneered at her, bouncing up and down again on the board. She heard a nearby lifeguard blow his whistle.

The next thing she knew, she lost her balance and was falling, falling down into the water. Splash!

CHAPTER 8

DON'T FALL
FOR THAT

Rosco jumped to his feet in alarm. His ears had perked up when he'd heard Jeffrey's sneering calls. He had seen the entire event from his spot in the shade. Izzy soon rose to the surface and swam to the edge of the pool, coughing and spitting water. She looked a bit stunned, but she wasn't hurt.

Rosco hurried over as she reached the edge of the pool. Izzy climbed out, and then burst into tears.

"That boy! He made me fall!" she said.

"I saw him yelling at you and standing on the board on your turn!" Madison said. "What was he saying?

"He was telling me to hurry up! But I was too scared to jump right away! I didn't want to be rushed," Izzy said, sobbing.

Rosco listened as the girls grew more and more upset.

By this time, Jeffrey had cannonballed off of the diving board, making a huge splash. He swam to the edge, then climbed out of the pool and stuck out his tongue at Izzy. "Bet you won't *fall* for that one again, ha? Get it, *fall*?"

A look of surprise came across her face. She couldn't believe he was making a joke of it. "I was going to jump, but you *made* me fall! I'm telling on you," she said.

Just then the lifeguard blew her whistle once more.

"Go ahead!" Jeffrey bragged. "I was only playing around. And you didn't get hurt. It's only water."

At this, Rosco took a few steps toward Jeffrey and began to growl softly.

"Aw, not you again, mutt," Jeffrey said.

Rosco growled a little louder.

The lifeguard blew her whistle again, signaling to get Jeffrey's attention. Jeffrey glanced up at her, sitting high on the lifeguard chair. She wasn't smiling.

"Stay right here until your counselor gets here, young man. Girls, can you wait here too?"

"Yes, ma'am," Natasha answered.

"Thank you." The lifeguard returned to watching the kids in the pool. Rosco sat down and waited with the girls.

Mandy suddenly noticed that something unusual was going on with three of her cabinmates, her dog, and a boy from James's cabin. She swam over to tell James, who was tossing a lightweight basketball into a poolside hoop with his friends. They quickly climbed out of the water and went to see what was happening.

The brother and sister pair walked up behind Rosco, just as Matt, one of James's counselors, approached the group.

"That boy shook the diving board until I fell off," Izzy explained.

Matt turned to Jeffrey with a stern look on his face. "Is this true?"

"Of course not," Jeffrey answered.

One of the younger girls spoke up. "He's lying. He did so."

Rosco growled again, this time baring his teeth at Jeffrey.

"I was just standing there on the ladder, waiting my turn," said Jeffrey. "She fell off."

Now Rosco let out a quiet, angry bark. Jeffrey backed up a step. "What's your dog's problem? What's he doing here, anyway?" Jeffrey said to James.

"He knows a lie when he hears one," said Mandy.

Matt raised his eyebrows at this and gave Jeffrey another of his stern looks. "What really happened, Jeffrey? Did you shake the diving board until this young lady fell off? Because we have rules here, so if you. . ."

Rosco stepped closer to Jeffrey and

growled some more.

"Can't you make the mutt stop?" he said to James.

"He won't leave you alone until you tell the truth," James told him.

"So what's the truth, Jeffrey?" the counselor said.

"All right, all right! I might've bounced a little on the other end of the board, but I was just running out of patience. She was taking *forever* to jump! I didn't know she would fall off!"

"Yes, you did," Izzy said. "You kept bouncing until I fell off, and then you made a joke out of it when you got out of the pool. I could've gotten hurt."

"Okay, I've heard enough," said Matt. "Jeffrey, you can sit out for the next fifteen minutes. And I'm keeping my eye on you. The rule is, only one person on the diving board at a time, no matter how long it takes to jump."

"Fine," Jeffrey said sharply.

James turned to walk away but stopped

to give Jeffrey a warning. "You'd better pick on someone your own size next time. Leave my sister and her friends alone."

Jeffrey shrugged his shoulders. "Whatever." He walked to the corner of the pool yard and sat down, pouting.

Izzy reached over and petted Rosco's soft head. "Your dog is the best, Mandy."

Just then, Sheriff walked up. The old dog was getting sick and tired of watching Rosco become everyone's favorite dog. He growled at Rosco, but Rosco understood what he meant. *Stay out of their business, you show-off.*

Rosco stared at Sheriff. He wasn't showing off. He'd had to step in and keep that boy honest.

Maybe if Sheriff wasn't so grouchy all the time, they'd want to pet him too. Rosco shook himself and returned to his shady spot under the tree. That old dog needed to lighten up.

James jumped in the pool and swam back to his friends.

"We've got to do something about Jeffrey," James said. He's causing trouble everywhere he goes. I'm afraid someone could get hurt if we don't stop him soon."

"But what can we do?" said Caleb, tossing the basketball to James. "He won't listen to us when we try to talk sense into him. And he doesn't listen to the counselors. He just takes his punishments and then makes more trouble later."

James passed the ball to Mike. He took a shot at the hoop. The ball missed. Mike said, "Well, what if we try and include him in our group, so he doesn't feel so left out? Then maybe he'll stop all this."

"That might work," Caleb said. "I don't know, though . . ." He retrieved the ball and passed it to James.

James aimed the ball and threw. "I guess it's worth a shot," he said. The ball circled the rim and plopped in.

CHAPTER 9
ICE CREAM SOCIAL

Despite the setbacks, the days began to pass at Camp Hickory Ridge full of activity and full of fun.

On Tuesday morning, Mandy's cabin group went on a two-mile hike around the lake. They climbed over boulders, spotted rabbits on the trail, and saw wild geese on the lake. Kimberly even picked up a frog they found on the trail near the water. It jumped out of her hands before anyone else got a turn to hold it.

On Tuesday afternoon, it was the seven-to-nine year old girls' turn for a lesson about lake safety, followed by a demonstration on how to row and steer a canoe. The girls paddled about on the lake in the hot sun for over an hour. It was the first time that Mandy and Kim had ever rowed a canoe by themselves. Margaret partnered with Izzy, while Madison and Natasha shared another canoe.

"This is hard work," Kim said, paddling back toward the dock. Her arms were getting very tired.

"You can say that again," Mandy agreed. But they both smiled.

* * *

James's week was turning around too. His cabin group shot archery on Tuesday morning. Mike and Tim were the only ones in the group to shoot a bull's-eye, but the rest of the boys looked forward to more practice later in the week.

That afternoon, the boys did a scavenger hunt that took them all over camp and the surrounding forest. James's team, composed of Mike, Caleb, and Jeffrey, found almost everything on the list: the sharp-edged rock, the hickory tree leaf, and even the bird feather.

Most of the other groups hadn't been able to find a feather. James's team came in second place.

Things were going pretty smoothly. Jeffrey hadn't played any more pranks on the boys since the snake incident. He had gladly sat at meals with James and his friends since they had asked him and had begun to reveal a more decent, likeable side to his personality.

James began to think that maybe Jeffrey could actually become their friend and that he would stay out of trouble for the rest of the week. He thought maybe Mike was right when he said that all Jeffrey needed was to be treated like a friend, in order to act like a friend.

After dinner, the children and counselors headed outside for dessert at the evening's all-camp Ice Cream Social, a build-your-own-sundae event.

There were three flavors of ice cream to choose from—chocolate, vanilla, and strawberry, all you could eat—and toppings of chocolate sauce and colored sprinkles. At the end of the buffet, there were canisters of spray whipped cream and cherries to top off the creations.

Rosco and Sheriff were even given bowls of vanilla ice cream. Mandy, Kim, and Margaret lined up with the rest of the girls from their cabin. The evening felt cheerful.

Caleb and James waited patiently behind Jeffrey for their sundaes. Finally, nearing the end of the buffet line, Jeffrey grabbed the canister of whipped cream.

"Look out, Caleb!" Jeffrey laughed. "You look like you need some of this!" He held it up to Caleb as if he'd squirt it all over his face.

Caleb quickly jerked his head away. "Cut it out, Jeffrey!"

But, in the process, Caleb backed up into James, stepped on James's foot, and lost his grip on his plastic bowl.

"Sorry, James!" Caleb said.

Then he saw his ice cream. His three-scoop sundae had splattered to the ground, spoon and all. Ice cream, sprinkles, and chocolate sauce blanketed the grass.

"Aw, man!" Caleb said. The three boys gazed at the mess.

"Oh, wow! Ooops! Sorry Caleb!" Jeffrey sneered, setting the canister back down on the table. "But wait, you thought I was really going to squirt you?"

"Yeah!"

"I wasn't. I was only joking!"

Sheriff quickly descended on the delicious mess, licking it up rapidly. Rosco skipped over too, but Sheriff growled at him. He wasn't sharing. *Stay back, Rosco.*

"Well, nice sundae, butterfingers!" Jeffrey teased.

Caleb huffed. "I didn't even get one bite!"

"I didn't drop it, you did!" Jeffrey replied.

"Here, Caleb," said James, stepping in.

"You can have mine. I'll go make another one. Just ignore him."

Caleb took it slowly, still a bit shocked at the mess on the ground that Sheriff was quickly devouring. "Thanks, James," he said gratefully, "but you don't have to . . ."

"No, take it, Caleb. It's okay," said James, giving Jeffrey a sharp look. "You'd better watch it, Jeffrey. You need to be more careful. And you shouldn't tease someone when they're already upset."

Jeffrey just shrugged and walked to the picnic table where the other boys from their cabin were sitting.

Caleb sat down next to Mike and quietly told him what had happened. They exchanged frustrated looks, shaking their heads.

"It doesn't seem to make a difference if we include him in our group or not," Caleb said, discouraged. "He's still going to make trouble."

CHAPTER 10

THE SHADOW ON THE WINDOW

After the sundaes were gone, the whole camp played a giant game of freeze tag. The boys were exhausted after such a busy day.

Later, at James's cabin, everyone got ready for bed. Matt made his usual announcement as he flipped the last light switch on the wall. "Lights out. Time to go to sleep, guys."

At Mandy's cabin, the scene was similar. The girls brushed their teeth and changed into their pajamas. They settled into their bunks, quietly chatting with one another, reading a book by flashlight, or writing a letter to their parents.

"Okay, girls. Lights out. It's quiet time now," said Jennifer. She switched off the lights and left the room. In the corner bunk, Izzy turned over inside of her sleeping bag. "I'm too tired to stay up, anyway." She yawned.

A little while later, most of the girls were asleep. Suddenly, a bright light appeared at the window beside Margaret's bunk. It was coming from outside. The light moved about unsteadily. Eerie shadows began to appear on the walls and floor inside the cabin.

"Look!" Kimberly whispered loudly. "What's that?"

"Eeeeeek!" Margaret screamed. Several other girls screamed.

"What is that?" Margaret pointed at a shadowy shape. She jumped out of her bed, which was on the lower bunk, and flitted away from the window.

Jennifer came racing in from the other room where the counselors slept. "What's going on in here?" she asked. "What's all the

screaming about?"

"Look! Over there!" Mandy cried. She pointed to the window beside Margaret's bed.

A strange and monstrous figure now seemed to be lurking just outside of it. The figure's shadowy movements twitched about on the glass pane.

Madison quickly climbed down from the top bunk, scrambling to escape the clutches of the spooky shadow.

"Hold on a minute, everyone!" Jennifer told them in a loud whisper. "I'll be right back!" She ran from the room. Another counselor quickly came into the girls' bunkroom to keep the girls calm.

The girls heard the screen door of the cabin slam shut as their counselor raced outside. Whoever was responsible for shining the flashlight outside the cabin would be caught red-handed.

Out on the porch, Rosco had been pacing about with worry. He had already heard the screams coming from inside Mandy's cabin, and was on high alert for any noise coming from the woods. As Jennifer jumped off the porch in pursuit of the shadowy figure, Rosco followed her.

But by the time the young woman and the dog reached the back of the cabin, the spooky shadows had stopped. Whoever was responsible for frightening the girls had disappeared.

"Doggone it! They got away! They must've heard me." Jennifer glanced at Rosco, then back at the woods. "Well, stay away, whoever you are!" she shouted into the dark, empty night.

She wasn't about to chase any young pranksters down the dark trail to the boys' cabins at this time of night.

But Rosco wouldn't let a troublemaker get away without a chase. On pure instinct, he raced off down the dark trail.

"Rosco, wait, it's okay!" Jennifer called. "It's probably just one of the boys!" But Rosco kept going.

Moments later, Jeffrey tiptoed in through the side door of his cabin. It was very dark in the bunkroom. A board creaked under his feet on the old wooden floor, but he slipped into his bed quietly. Most of the boys were already asleep, but some were not.

Caleb sat up and leaned on his elbows.

"Where were you?" he whispered.

"Nowhere," Jeffrey lied. "Just went to the bathroom."

"Yeah, sure you did," James said. "Then you're not responsible for all that screaming we just heard way off in the distance?"

"No way," Jeffrey said, climbing into bed and smiling to himself. "Not me." He was glad it was dark, because he couldn't keep from grinning. He had pulled it off—his practical joke had worked!

"Right," said James sarcastically, turning to face the wall in his sleeping bag. "Sure, you're not." He didn't believe him for a second.

Jeffrey just shrugged.

James sighed. Here we go again, he thought. More pranks and lies—from one of the oldest kids in our cabin, no less! Treating him like a friend definitely wasn't stopping him from making trouble. What were they going to do about this kid?

CHAPTER 11
WORRIES

Mandy stared at the ceiling. She was wide awake. It was late, and most of the girls were asleep. But she just couldn't seem to settle down. She had been tossing and turning all night, trying to chase away the scary thoughts.

It didn't help that Jennifer had explained that it was just the boys playing a joke on the girls and that it happened every year. She still couldn't block the fear from her mind.

Even though Rosco had come back safely from the woods and had found no one out there, she couldn't stop worrying. Mandy wondered what could have happened to him out there, late at night, if he hadn't come right back. What if there were real monsters?

No, she knew better than that. Monsters weren't real. Mandy wasn't normally afraid of the dark. But now, the dark seemed like a bad place. And those scary thoughts made her miss her parents. And missing her parents made her miss the safety of her own bed. And missing her own bed made her homesick.

Those sad feelings started to creep back into her brain. She turned over again in her sleeping bag, trying to find a comfortable enough position in which to fall asleep. She squeezed her eyes shut and tried to think good thoughts.

Just calm down, she told herself. Everything's fine. Her mother always told her that she should think good thoughts as she fell asleep at night, especially when she was worried that she might have nightmares.

Thinking good thoughts helped to scare away all the bad thoughts and give her good dreams. She'd better give it a try.

* * *

Rosco, on the other hand, was exhausted. He had run all the way to the boys' unit, and sniffed for clues around each of the three, large cabins where the boys slept. He had picked up the scent of one boy in particular.

He knew he'd heard someone running off down the trail. He was sure he'd heard the sound of only one person's footsteps.

Rosco just wished he'd chased the boy sooner and not waited for Jennifer to come out of the cabin first. He might've caught up to the troublemaker if he'd left sooner. But he hadn't. Whichever boy had scared the girls had gotten away.

When Rosco returned to Mandy's cabin twenty minutes later, Mandy rushed out to greet him.

"Thank goodness you're back, Rosco!" Mandy said. "Jennifer said it was probably just some boys playing a nasty joke on us! I'm so glad you're okay! That was very brave of you!"

Jennifer had explained it all to them. She said that it was nothing to worry about. But Rosco still thought he'd like to know exactly who did it. And he had a pretty good idea just who it might be—someone who'd already caused problems this week for lots of other kids—someone in James's cabin.

* * *

Back at the boys' cabin, James also lay awake thinking. Didn't Jeffrey realize that if he kept this up, he could get kicked out of camp? Was playing pranks really worth it to miss out on the rest of the week?

In some ways, James hoped Jeffrey *would* get kicked out of camp because he was so tired of the problems that Jeffrey caused.

Jeffrey just didn't seem to *get* it. Wasn't it enough that they were treating him like one of their group now? He must not have any idea what it means to be a real friend. Not after what he did to Caleb tonight at the ice cream party, even if it *had been* an accident. None of that would've happened if Jeffrey hadn't been goofing around.

And now Jeffrey had played a prank on Mandy's cabin. James had specifically told him to leave his sister and her friends alone.

When would Jeffrey stop all this nonsense, stop making everyone feel uneasy? Each boy in James's cabin worried that he'd be the target of Jeffrey's next practical joke.

It only takes one bad apple to spoil the bunch, his mother always said. Well, that certainly was turning out to be true. James didn't want any more of his week to be ruined by this kid's rotten behavior.

They'd have to do more than include Jeffrey in their group. They'd have to keep an eye on him, at all times. They'd have to stick close to him, keep track of what he was doing. He'd talk to Caleb and Mike tomorrow. Together, they would put a lid on this can of worms.

CHAPTER 12

CAPTURE THE FLAG

Soon Thursday evening arrived. It was the biggest night of the week—the evening that the whole camp played a giant game of capture the flag. It was the best game in the world, at least as far as James was concerned.

He and his friends had the freedom to roam the entire camp *and* the woods without a counselor leading them around. James had been looking forward to it all week.

Each cabin group arrived at the main lawn outside the dining hall. The kids were split into two teams: blue and red, and were given a bandana in their team color to tie around their heads. James, Caleb, and Mike were on the blue team together. Jeffrey was put on their team also, but the boys were glad. This way they could keep an eye on him, now that they thought for sure that he couldn't be trusted.

Excited to play the game for the first time, Mandy, Margaret, and Kimberly were on the blue team, also. Even the dogs were placed on teams, with bandanas wrapped around their necks in place of their collars. Rosco's was blue because Mandy was on the blue team; Sheriff's was red so there would be one dog on each team.

The object of the game was simple: to capture the other team's flag hidden inside their territory and to bring it all the way back to one's own territory without getting tagged.

The rules were also simple. If kids were tagged, they were taken to the other team's jail. The jails were picnic tables in the corners of the grassy field in each team's territory.

Prisoners had to sit at the picnic tables until freed by a member of their own team who made it safely across enemy lines and retagged them.

A boundary line was made using orange cones. The entire camp was divided into two territories. Team members weren't allowed to hide inside of cabins or other buildings. But everywhere else was allowed, including the forest and the sports field and the outsides of buildings.

The head counselor, Tony, announced the rules over a megaphone.

"At the end of two hours the game will be over. If neither team captures a flag by then, the team with the fewest members in jail will be the winner. And just since it's looking a little overcast this evening, I want to tell you all that just in case there's any bad weather this evening, everyone should head back to the dining hall porch for shelter immediately. We'll postpone the game until tomorrow if that happens."

The counselors were to spread out across camp during the game, just to make sure that everyone was following the rules and playing safely.

"So here we go!" Tony blew hard on the whistle. "Go capture those flags!"

James, Caleb, and Jeffrey followed Mike into the woods at a brisk pace. "Come on! We need to get out of view so we can make a plan!" Mike called.

Mandy and her friends scattered into the open field, crossing the boundary line. This seemed like the most direct way to find the other team's flag.

Out in the field, several members of the red team descended upon the younger girls instantly. Kimberly and Margaret made a mad dash toward the center of the grass but were quickly overtaken.

"Gotcha!" said a couple of twelve-year-old girls from the red team. "Off to jail!" one girl said to the other. "I'll take them! Hands behind your backs, girls!" She grabbed them roughly by their wrists but smiled. "Don't worry," she whispered. "I'm only playing tough. Jail is fun in this game!" Margaret and

Kim peeked at each other, grinning.

But Mandy got away, having run back behind blue lines, alone, when her friends were caught. She ran to the edge of the field and headed quickly toward the lake trail. Now she was safely in her own territory. Sure, she was alone—even Rosco had run off in the other direction—but at least she'd gotten away.

James had told her to look out for the defenders on the other team. They'd catch her quickly if she entered enemy territory out in the open.

Nearing one of the cabins by the lake trail, Mandy stopped to take a breath. "Whew!" She stepped closer to the cabin, to stay out of view.

No one's around, she thought, glancing cautiously past the cabin for any red team members to tag. She'd better keep moving. And somehow she'd have to reach the red team's jail, so she could free her friends. But how would she get over there without getting caught?

Just then she heard quick footsteps approaching. It was three boys from the red team. Two boys from her team were chasing them. And Rosco, wearing the blue bandana that James had tied around his neck, was close behind! The boys ran on but Rosco stopped when he saw Mandy.

"Hey, buddy. How ya' doin'?" Mandy

said, petting his back. Rosco panted, smiling at her. Then he perked up his ears, looking back toward the woods at something that caught his attention.

"You're having a good time, aren't you, boy?" Rosco panted and smiled some more. "Okay then, go on. Run with those kids. I'm fine. Go on!"

Rosco waited a moment, wondering whether or not Mandy was telling him the truth. She would've told him if anything was wrong, wouldn't she?

"Go on, boy! I'm off to free my friends from jail!" she said. "I'll call for you if I need you, as loud as I can." She smiled.

Rosco was really enjoying this game. There were so many kids who wanted to run with him and so many kids to chase. This was the most fun he'd had at camp yet.

He studied Mandy's face. She didn't seem worried or troubled at all. Deciding to believe her, he raced off into the forest to rejoin the boys on his team.

Mandy smiled and followed the lake trail deeper into the woods. She would cut across the underbrush, off the trail, and cross into red territory before anyone would notice. She was sure it wouldn't take long.

CHAPTER 13
THE PLAN

Inside the woods, Mike led his group of four to an empty spot below a large hickory tree. He pulled out a folded-up piece of paper. It was a map of camp.

The staff kept a pile of maps in the office for directing new kids to their cabins on the first day of each new session of camp. Mike's parents had left theirs with him. Mike pointed to the map.

"Here's the archery range, and over here is the lean-to that the older kids built last summer, next to the lake. Matt told me that it's still standing. It's right off of this trail, not very far from this, and it's in blue territory," he said, pointing to an X he had drawn.

"If any of us gets separated and can't find another one of our group, let's meet at the lean-to."

"What's a lean-to?" asked Jeffrey.

"It's a small shelter built out of branches and sticks, covered with leaves. It looks kind of like a tent."

"Oh, okay," said Jeffrey.

Mike looked up. "So, are we in agreement on the plan?" The other boys nodded.

"But what if one of us gets tagged and taken to jail?" Jeffrey asked.

"If that happens, don't worry. Since this game goes on for two whole hours, you're pretty likely to be freed by someone on our team," Mike said. "Even if it's not one of us. But we'll each promise to do our best to try and free each other, right?"

"Right," James and Caleb answered.

"Okay, I agree, then," Jeffrey said.

"Now, we've got to get over to enemy territory and find that flag. Let's stick together unless someone gets caught. But listen, if anyone does get caught," Mike said intently, looking at Jeffrey, "don't give away the rest of our positions. The rest of us will be hiding. Just go to jail. It won't do us any good if we all get caught."

"Got it," Jeffrey said. James and Caleb nodded.

"You sure, Jeffrey? No funny business, right?" Mike said.

Jeffrey nodded. He became very serious.

"I'm sure."

The other boys glanced at each other, deciding to believe him. Jeffrey really seemed to want to play by the rules. He seemed to be telling the truth when he agreed to stick to the plan. Still, they would keep a close eye on him.

"All right, let's head toward red territory," James said. "Keep your heads down."

So the boys quietly moved deeper into the woods, into red territory, far from the grassy field where the red team's defenders were waiting to tag people.

"Where can that flag be?" James said quietly to Mike. The rules said the flag had to be visible, even if it wasn't in an obvious place. It had to be around here somewhere.

Carefully, the boys edged forward, searching the bases of trees and moss-covered rocks.

"Keep your heads down," James whispered. "We can get tagged here."

Mike, James, Caleb, and Jeffrey, working

together, were still unnoticed by any members of the red team. They spread out and were stepping quietly on the underbrush as they searched for the flag.

Suddenly, the sound of cracking twigs and crunching leaves came from close behind Caleb. Fast footsteps followed.

"Get them!" a boy called, approaching rapidly. Two more boys from the red team jumped out from behind trees and bushes. They raced at the blue team.

"Run!" Mike screamed. But quickly, Mike and James were overtaken. Their captors grabbed each of them by an elbow and took them out onto the trail. Still free, Caleb ran in the other direction but tripped over a log and fell to his knees. The third boy ran up and tagged him.

"What about that other kid? The taller one with the brown hair," one of the red team said. "There were four of them."

"Oh, he won't get far by himself in the woods. Let's take these ones to jail first. Then we'll come back and get him."

But Jeffrey had gotten away. He'd run as fast as his legs would take him. He'd found a hiding place behind a cluster of large rocks. He would stay hidden until the boys were gone, just like Mike had told them to do.

Jeffrey was proud of himself. He was the only one fast enough to get away! He could go free his friends from jail and put them back in the game.

But wait, what about the flag? It had to be out here somewhere. They'd already searched so much red territory. If he went to free the guys from jail, someone else might come along and find it, and take all the glory, after all of their hard work.

Jeffrey wanted that glory. But he also wanted to do this for James and the guys. They were treating him like a friend, despite the tricks he had played on them all.

More than that, he was sure he could do this on his own. He'd be fine out here in the woods by himself. He thought, surely, that with some luck, he could find the flag before anyone else and manage to get away from any red team defenders that might come along. He was older than Caleb, James, and Mike anyway. He was bigger and stronger.

He could become the hero of the blue team if he could capture that flag. Then all the kids on his team would like him. Yes, he would do it. Someone else would have to free the guys from jail.

Quietly Jeffrey moved forward, inspecting every possible hiding place for the flag.

CHAPTER 14

WHERE THERE'S THUNDER

In another part of the forest, Mandy looked about. She knew where she was and figured she was probably still in blue territory. But she was starting to get worried.

She had walked a long way from the lake trail into the woods, trying to sneak across the red side and come out right behind the red jail. She knew she would've gotten caught if she'd run straight toward the red jail from the field.

Now, she thought she was finally in red territory, but she had been all by herself for some time now. It was getting lonely and a little creepy.

Suddenly, a few girls from the red team ran by, chasing some boys from the blue team. Yep, it looked like she must be in red territory now. She ducked down behind a tree.

Maybe she should go back to the field where the blue team defenders would be. Maybe she should try to free Kim and Margaret by running straight down the grassy field instead of sneaking around the outside. Maybe she should just go ahead and get caught and get put in jail with her friends. She'd never been this far out in this forest before, alone. She just wasn't sure what to do...

Just then, a soft rumbling began in the distance. Was that thunder? She brushed off the thought. No, it was probably just her imagination.

But it began again, this time a little louder.

Uh oh.

The sky had grown darker with each

minute. But Mandy hadn't noticed it very much, walking through the forest where the trees blocked out most of the sky.

Now she heard a loud clapping sound. It was indeed thunder, and it sounded closer than the last time.

A small drizzle dampened her hair. Another loud thunderclap boomed, then another, then another! Immediately, hard, fast rain began to fall.

Oh no, Mandy thought. She didn't like thunder. Because where there was thunder, there was lightning! She felt a sinking feeling in her stomach. She peered out toward the lake, where she could see a little bit more of the sky.

Hard rain was splattering off of the smooth surface of the lake. A bright light flashed for a quick second. Lightning! Then another loud thunderclap boomed.

What should she do? Where should she go? She was all by herself!

She had no choice. Mandy began

running, quickly, back to camp through red territory. She jumped over rocks and twigs on the trail. She didn't care if someone tagged her! Not that they would anyway, in this weather!

She just wanted to find shelter and be near other people. Her heart pounded so fast she thought it might burst.

Back at the field, rain poured down by the bucket loads! James, Mike, and Caleb had run from the picnic table jail with the rest of the captured blue team campers as soon as the thunder had started. They'd all headed straight for the dining hall porch, which wasn't far off, but they'd still gotten soaked.

Kids from all over camp were steadily streaming back now. Some were muddy. All were drenched. The game of capture the flag would have to wait until the rain stopped.

But, for all of the kids who were safely under a roof by now, the storm was exciting! It was the best kind of summer storm—the kind in which puddle jumping, splashing, and sopping wet clothing and hair brought laughter and fun.

The thunder and lightning had stopped. Now they just had steady, fast rain.

"I hope Mandy's okay!" Margaret said.

James had come over, asking if they

knew where his sister was.

"I'm sure she'll be back soon. Don't worry. She'll be fine!" Kim answered, sticking her head out from under the porch and holding out her tongue to catch some raindrops.

"She's probably with Natasha or some of our other cabinmates by now," Margaret said. "I saw her run off into the woods when we got caught at the start." Margaret laughed and stuck her tongue out to catch raindrops, too.

Luckily, Mandy was indeed fine. She had just come out of the woods and was crossing the grassy lawn. The dining hall was in sight and the lights inside it were shining warmly. She smiled in relief as she watched her fellow campers playing in the rain.

Thank goodness, she thought. I'm safe now. She was proud of herself for acting on her instincts and for not wasting any time. She had not allowed her fear to take over her actions. She had not frozen up and cried for help out in the woods. She'd used her perfectly good legs and gotten out on her own. And she had done all of that without wishing that her mother and father were there to save her. She'd been caught in a thunderstorm, alone, in the woods, and had handled it by herself! That was really something, she thought!

* * *

Back out in the woods, Jeffrey had made a different choice. He, too, was alone. He had heard some kids hollering to each other as they dashed back to camp when the rain started. "Let's go! Run!"

He could've followed them.

But even though he was supposed to go to the dining hall if it rained, he realized he wasn't far from the lean-to on the map. In a few moments, he'd thought it over and made his decision. He would make a run for it. He would head to the lean-to.

That's really what a lean-to must be for,

he reasoned—to take shelter from the rain. He might as well use it. Why bother going all the way back to the dining hall? He'd go wait at the lean-to until the rain stopped, even though he knew the rules.

Jeffrey knew that when the rain stopped, he'd probably be the only one left out here in the woods. That would give him a clear advantage to cross quickly back into red territory without getting caught. Then he could find the flag before anyone else did.

He could win the game for his team and be the hero—despite a downpour, despite breaking the rule about going back in bad weather.

After all, no one would know that he stayed out here during the storm, would they? Nah, the rain would probably stop quickly and the game would start up again before the counselors could take a headcount and notice he was missing.

He *could* still be the hero. Then, everyone would finally like him.

Jeffrey picked up his pace. He took shortcuts off of the trail, stepping across small rocks and stumbling through the wet underbrush. Thunder echoed over the thick cover of the trees. Lightning lit up the sky. He wiped raindrops from his brow.

In another moment Jeffrey stopped. A cluster of boulders stood in front of him. The huge rocks were stacked up as big as a small

hill, and they looked a bit slippery.

On both sides of the boulders, bushes and trees blocked any sort of walkway. It looked easier to climb up and over the rocks than to squeeze around them. A stream of water had formed because of the rain and was running down the hill next to the boulders, toward the lake.

Jeffrey had two choices—either cross the boulders or go back and find another, probably longer, route to the lean-to. Jeffrey's heart raced.

All right, he thought. He could do this. Carefully, Jeffrey stepped onto the rocks and began to make his way across them slowly, trying not to slip. He held on to the rocky ground at times, keeping a grip on the higher rocks as his feet found the best spots on which to step as he climbed higher.

Rain still poured down, but the trees blocked some of the effects of the water. It only felt like light rain inside the forest.

Jeffrey had made it about halfway up the

rocks when a loud clap of thunder startled him. Out of instinct, he ducked, but that made him slip. In an instant, one foot slid sharply down into the narrow space between two large rocks.

"Ouch!" he cried. Pulling hard, he tried to force his foot out of the tight crevice. But it wouldn't move. His leg was inside the narrow space up to his knee, and his high-top sneaker was stuck! "Oh no!"

Jeffrey looked around. It was still raining and thundering, and no one would be coming to help. The counselors would have a hard enough time accounting for all of the kids who were spread out around camp during the storm.

There would probably be lots of confusion because some kids would take more than getting back than others.

So, it would be a long while before they would notice that he was missing. And he was far away from the last place that James, Mike, and Caleb had seen him, so they wouldn't even know where to look, unless they remembered the lean-to plan. But now he couldn't even get *there*! What was he going to do? He'd have to find a way to get unstuck by himself.

He pulled again, harder this time. "Ouch!" His shoe was not budging. Plus, since it was a high-top sneaker, laced all the way up to the top of his ankle, he couldn't pull his foot out of the shoe.

The hole between the rocks was long and skinny, so reaching down to untie those laces wouldn't be easy.

But he'd have to give it a try. Struggling, he squeezed a few fingers down into the hole toward his laces.

CHAPTER 15
BETTER GO INVESTIGATE

Rosco hurried on through the forest, his paws soaking wet and caked in mud. Raindrops pitter-pattered off of his thick black and brown coat. A little rain never bothered him.

He had wandered deep into the woods, first, following some kids on the blue team who'd been chasing some kids on the red team.

Then, when they'd dragged the red team players off to jail, he'd heard some squirrels in the underbrush and raced off to find them. The squirrels had gotten away, but in the process, Rosco had ventured much farther from camp than most of the kids had. That's when the storm began.

So, now he was heading back, off-trail. It was quicker that way, to take a few shortcuts through the ferns and underbrush. Soon he saw the large pile of boulders that he'd crossed on his way in.

But this time someone was sitting on top of the boulders, shouting for help. It looked like one of the kids. He'd better go investigate.

Rosco hopped from rock to rock, higher and higher, trying not to slide across the slippery surfaces, until he reached the flat-topped boulder where the child sat.

So, it was Jeffrey, Rosco thought, staring at him now—troublemaker, prankster, Jeffrey, shouting desperately for help, tears streaming down his face. The boy who had scared the girls in Mandy's cabin, the boy who would have been partly to blame if Rosco had been run down by a windsurfer, the boy who had shaken the diving board until Mandy's bunkmate fell off—this was the kid who was crying like a baby and needed his help.

Jeffrey wiped his eyes quickly when he saw the dog.

"I—I didn't hear you, Rosco, with all this rain. How . . . I mean—where did you come from?" he stuttered with embarrassment, choking back sobs.

Rosco stood tall, studying him, thinking hard.

"I—I'm stuck," Jeffrey said. "My foot—I mean, my shoe . . . I stepped down in here by accident and my shoe got trapped between the rocks. And now I can't get out!" He started to sob again. "And the rain won't stop, and nobody can hear me! I don't know what to do! Can you help me, boy? Can you?"

Rosco looked around, scanning the area beyond the large rocks. Jeffrey couldn't tell if he would come to his aid or not.

"Oh man, why am I talking to a dog anyway? What good would that do?" Jeffrey said. "You're not going to help me, anyway."

Rosco tilted his head, listening closely. There he goes again, Rosco thought—the sharp tongue. This kid deserves a lot worse after all he's done to make trouble. Maybe feeling helpless will teach him a lesson or two.

The large shepherd climbed back down carefully over the rocks and onto the ground. He'd be right back.

But Jeffrey didn't understand. "You're leaving me? Aw, man! I knew you wouldn't help me! You're just a dumb dog! Go ahead, leave me alone out here! I don't need you, mutt! I don't need anyone!" Jeffrey sobbed.

But Rosco was only looking for a stick. He wasn't leaving Jeffrey, no matter how many names the boy might call him; no matter how many nasty tricks he'd played on the kids this week. Jeffrey was still a child that needed help. And Rosco was always willing to help.

After a short search, Rosco found a big stick. It was about two feet long, thick enough

and strong enough for what he had in mind. Rosco picked it up and dragged it back up onto the tall boulder where Jeffrey sat.

Jeffrey stared in shock at Rosco's return. "You're back?"

Rosco dropped the stick in front of the boy.

"And, is that for me?" Jeffrey said. An apologetic look crossed his face.

Jeffrey picked it up and looked at it for a minute, trying to decide what he could do with it. "Thanks, I guess?" He poked it about on the rock, soon realizing it might fit down into the crevice. He lowered it carefully. It did fit!

Jeffrey had an idea. He could push on his heel with the stick. He tried it. The shoe loosened ever so slightly. He tried to wiggle his foot, again pushing on his heel with the stick, forcing it forward, toward the wider part of the gap in the rock.

Rosco stood by and watched nervously. If this didn't work, he wasn't sure what to do next, except go back to camp to get help.

But little by little, the shoe was moving. It *was* working!

It didn't take long until the shoe had moved far enough forward for Jeffrey to wiggle it out the rest of the way. At last, he was free! He lifted his foot out of the hole and brought it up next to his other foot. Finally, he sat comfortably on the rock, sighing with relief.

"I did it! I'm not stuck! I just needed a push! Rosco, I did it!"

He looked at the dog, who was smiling widely, tongue hanging out. "I mean *we* did it! You saved me!"

Rosco barked triumphantly.

"Thanks, Rosco! What a smart boy you are! I'm so sorry I didn't trust you. I'm so sorry I yelled at you."

Rosco moved closer to Jeffrey and nudged him on the shoulder with his wet nose. Jeffrey reached over and petted him softly on the head. Rosco licked Jeffrey's hand to tell him that it was okay. He could forgive the boy.

"I'm sorry for being such a jerk this week." Jeffrey sighed. "You didn't *have* to help me. Thank you for getting me out of this mess. I promise I'll be nicer to you from now on."

CHAPTER 16
SHERIFF THE SPY

Not far away, from behind a bush, a large bullmastiff watched with great interest. He wore a red bandana around his wide neck. His sturdy paws were covered in mud, and his thin brown fur was soaking wet.

Sheriff had been out in the woods with some campers from his team when the storm hit. He was heading back home when he'd heard the boy's shouts and went to investigate. He was quite surprised when Rosco arrived at the boulder hill at the same time, just a few steps ahead of him.

Rosco had been too concerned with Jeffrey to notice Sheriff.

So, Sheriff, curious to see what Rosco

might do, had stayed hidden and witnessed the whole scene.

Well, how about that? The oversized pup must be more intelligent and gracious than he'd thought.

Watching Rosco think quickly and help the boy, especially since it was the same boy who'd played nasty tricks on the other kids all week, well, that sure took something, all right, Sheriff figured.

Sheriff had taken note of Jeffrey's lack of character all week. He knew Rosco could've easily left the boy there to fend for himself, considering the trouble he'd caused for James and Mandy.

He could've even taken the easy route and just gone back to camp to alert the counselors by barking and then taken them to Jeffrey. He could've let *them* deal with the boy.

But that would've caused Jeffrey even more embarrassment. And it would've left him out in the rain, all alone, for an even longer time, scared and helpless. No, Rosco definitely handled things in the most considerate way.

Sheriff thought that he just might need to give Rosco a second chance. Maybe he's not so bad. Maybe Sheriff had been silly to think that Rosco would want to take over his territory. Rosco sure didn't seem to want to take over anything, if Sheriff really thought about it.

Sheriff watched as Jeffrey and Rosco climbed down the rocks. Well, gosh, now would be as good a time as any, he thought. He waited until they reached the trail, and then ran to catch up to them.

"Well, hey Sheriff, what are you doing out here?" Jeffrey said in surprise, stopping. "We thought you'd be back at camp by now with everyone else."

Sheriff stood there, panting, looking at them. His long tongue stuck out. A little drool escaped from his chops. But his mouth turned upward, almost in a smile.

What's gotten into him? Rosco thought.

Jeffrey reached over and petted Sheriff softly on the back. "Come on, boy, we're heading back to camp. Walk with us."

Sheriff fell in line next to Rosco as they followed the trail. Rosco glanced his way, and this time Sheriff really did smile, in the way that only dogs can smile. "Ruff," Sheriff said. *All right, Rosco, let's head back.*

CHAPTER 17
NO MORE CLASS CLOWN

Jeffrey thought about the last hour as they walked. He'd better not push his luck. He'd head back to camp. His counselors had probably noticed he was missing by now. Even if that flag were still out here, he'd better forget about it.

Maybe he could still help his team find the flag and win the game after the rain stopped. That was better than sneaking around and trying to do it by himself, especially when he was supposed to be back at camp by now.

Thankfully, the rain had slowed down. Soon, Jeffrey and the dogs crossed the grassy field and arrived at the dining hall's covered porch. James, Caleb, and Mike hurried over to greet him.

"Jeffrey, where have you been? We were starting to worry!" James said. "Matt's been asking where you were. And Rosco and Sheriff, you're back, too! Hi, boys!" He patted the dogs on the back.

Jeffrey told them his story about the rocks and his shoe and Rosco. The boys listened closely, amazed.

"Guys," Jeffrey said. "Look, I know I should've come back when the rain started. But I wanted to find that flag so I could win the game for our team."

"We understand, Jeffrey," James said.

Jeffrey continued. "And I know if I had come to free you guys from jail, I never would've been out there alone and gotten stuck. I guess I deserved what happened. I let you down."

"Nah, it's okay," Mike said. "It's no big deal. The rain started anyway. We weren't in jail for very long."

"But I didn't come to free you like we agreed," Jeffrey went on. "And I guess I got very, very lucky that Rosco came along when he did. He really helped me out of a tight spot."

The boys smiled.

"But guys, I'm not stupid. I know that you've all been hanging out with me lately just because you wanted to keep an eye on me, so I wouldn't play any more pranks on you. But, as it turned out, I liked hanging out with you guys, and I liked being treated like I was your friend. So I wanted to win this game for all of us. I wanted you guys and everyone else to like me, finally."

The three boys listened in surprise.

"I wanted to do the right thing," Jeffrey went on. "I guess I was just going about it the wrong way. I should've played by the rules."

"That *is* true," Caleb answered. "Because it wouldn't have counted if you had captured the flag but broken the rule about returning in bad weather. The counselors would have said it was a forfeit, and we would've lost anyway."

"So I guess it all worked out for the best, then?" James said brightly. "The rain saved us from having to forfeit the game."

"I guess so," Jeffrey agreed. "But wait. I only played jokes on you because I wanted you to like me." He looked at the ground and shuffled his feet nervously. "Although it didn't really work."

"Well, Jeffrey, your jokes are sometimes mean, not funny," Mike replied.

"I know. I'm sorry about that," Jeffrey said. "But can you give me another chance? Can I still be a part of your group? I'll stop playing jokes, and I'll try really hard not to be rude or aim things at your face when you're holding tall bowls of ice cream." He smiled apologetically at Caleb.

"Of course, you can still be a part of our group," James said.

Caleb nodded. "See, camp is a place

where people are nice to each other, where you don't have to play jokes on people to make them like you. We're all friends here. You don't have to be a class clown just to fit in. I hope that you know that now."

A few other boys from their cabin had gathered around by this time and were listening.

"Just no more hiding that rubber snake in my bed," Tim said.

"Okay," Jeffrey answered.

"And you'd better swear you won't sneak the candy bars from my care packages anymore," said a boy named Jeremiah.

"I swear."

"And you'd better not throw me in the pool again!" said Josh.

"Me neither!" said Tim.

"Aw, come on. I can't even throw anyone in the pool?" Jeffrey grinned. "What fun *can* I have here?"

"All right, all right! You can still throw us in the pool!" Mike said. "But we're going to get you back if you do! Let's show him, guys!"

Mike reached over and wrapped both arms around Jeffrey's waist. With a lively smirk, he picked him up and carried him out into the rain, dropping him in a large puddle.

"This is what you're going to get if you throw anyone in the pool!" Mike said, jumping on him like it was a game of tackle football. The rest of the boys piled on.

Eventually, they all stood up again, laughing, muddy, and soaking wet.

Jeffrey wasn't angry. "I guess I deserved that!" he said. "But all right, I get it! I'll only throw you in the pool if I want to get thrown in too!"

Finally, when everyone's patience had just about run out, the rain slowed to a light drizzle and then stopped. The shy evening sun shone behind the last remaining clouds.

"It stopped!" the campers cheered. Several ran out onto the grass to see for themselves. "The rain finally stopped!"

A few minutes later, Tony pulled out his megaphone. "Sorry, campers, but capture the flag will be postponed until tomorrow afternoon. Everyone should return to their cabins now to dry off and settle in for the night."

The sun would be setting soon, and they all knew it was getting too late to go back out woods again, anyway. James was ___ed that their team would get a second ___ance tomorrow.

Friday afternoon arrived. Campers and counselors lined up to tie their bandanas on again. The flags were hidden—in new places this time—and the whistle was blown. The game began as it did the night before—same teams, same boundaries, same rules.

But this time, Mandy and her friends headed straight toward the lake trail and into the woods. "Come on, I know how we can sneak into red territory and look for the flag!" Mandy told them.

"Okay! And let's stay out of jail this time!" Margaret added.

Rosco followed. He would keep close by Mandy and the girls this afternoon.

* * *

Over in another part of the woods, James and his friends ran through their new plan.

"Okay," said Mike. "James, you and Caleb will go on defense in blue territory like we all decided. Catch as many red players as you can."

James and Caleb nodded, excited to chase down other players this time.

"Jeffrey and I will go on offense. We'll head to the red team's woods and search for the flag. When the horn sounds to let everyone know that the game is halfway over, we should all head to the lean-to. If any of us doesn't show up, we'll know that person's in jail and we need to go free them."

Caleb added, "But if you hear someone on the megaphone, that means that one of the teams won and the game is over. So head back to the field where the game started if you hear it."

"Right. Has everyone got it?" Mike asked.

"Got it," they answered. Then they split in pairs and parted ways.

It didn't take long for two boys looking for the blue flag to appear, sneaking along the path.

"Let's get em when they get close!" Caleb whispered to James from where they hid behind a rock. Caleb waited a few seconds, then jumped out and quickly tagged one red team boy. James tagged the other. "Off to jail, guys!"

Soon, Mandy's group, following the lake trail quietly through red territory, noticed a tall hickory tree with a small pile of rocks at the bottom of its trunk, about twenty feet from the trail. "Let's go check out that pile of rocks, guys," Mandy said. "That looks kind of strange."

"Keep your heads down," Margaret warned. "The red defenders will be waiting out here for blue players like us to come by."

"Hey, look! Footprints!" Kimberly said. Everyone stopped. "They go all the way from the trail to those rocks over there."

Yesterday's rain had left the ground still muddy today, so these footprints were easy to spot, especially since they went off the trail.

The girls and Rosco left the trail to inspect the footprints and the rocks, with Rosco close behind. But nothing seemed unusual about the rocks.

Mandy circled to the other side of the tree trunk as the others bent down to study the prints. All of a sudden she opened her mouth in surprise. "Guys! Look!" she said in a loud whisper. They hurried over. She pointed, placing one finger to her mouth. "Shhh."

There, on the other side of the tree, planted firmly in the dirt, stood a small red flag on a short, thin stick. It wasn't visible from the trail. It wasn't exactly hidden, but it didn't stand out either. The red team had done a good job of placing their important little treasure in a hiding spot, while strictly following the rule about keeping it visible.

"The flag! Oh, my gosh! It's the flag!"

CHAPTER 19
ROSCO KNOWS THE WAY

Mandy quickly pulled the red flag from the dirt. "They must've made this pile of rocks so they wouldn't forget where they hid the flag. Since all these trees look so much alike . . ."

"That's probably right!" Kimberly whispered. "But listen, we have to go before the guards see us! Hurry! They must be right around here somewhere!"

The rules stated that flag defenders, also called guards, were required to stay at least fifty feet from their own flag until an enemy invaded the area where the flag was hidden.

The girls and Rosco turned and began

scuffling through the dense underbrush toward the trail as quietly as they could.

But three red guards had spotted the group.

"Get them!" a cry came from the trees. It sounded like older kids—bigger faster, older kids, maybe twelve- or thirteen-year-old girls.

"Run!" Mandy screamed. She held tightly on to the flag.

They could hear the big kids catching up to them quickly. Mandy had to think fast.

She stopped and held the flag out to Rosco. "Here, boy! Take the flag! Take it back to camp, straight to the grassy field. Go past the orange cones to get to the blue side. Don't stop until you get there!"

Rosco took the flag from her, grasping the stick firmly in his teeth. He could do this. He was faster than any human. He knew exactly where to go. He dashed off, quickly reached the lake trail, and headed back toward camp.

In that short space of time, the red

guards caught up to the girls. Mandy was tagged first because she'd paused to give Rosco his orders.

"Go, Rosco! Good boy! Good boy!" Mandy called. In a few more seconds, he was out of sight.

"Someone's got to stop the dog!" one of the older girls called.

"I'm going!" said another. Off she ran.

"Me too!" said the third. The first guard quickly overtook Kim and Margaret.

"The rest of you are going to jail!" she said.

"Why bother?" Kim asked, defiantly, but a little out of breath. Mandy's dog is going to win this game for us. You might as well let us go now."

"That dog's not going to know what to do with the flag, or where to take it! He'll probably just drop it somewhere along the way when he hears a squirrel in the bushes. He won't make it back to blue territory on his own, not without one of us catching him first!" she warned. "We've got red players everywhere in these woods. So, it's off to jail with you three! This game's not over yet!"

But the girl had badly misjudged the fleeing dog. Rosco *did* know what to do with the flag, and he knew exactly where to take it. He raced down the lake trail back to camp. Among Rosco's many talents, speed and intelligence were at the top of the list.

* * *

Having no luck in their quest for the flag, Mike and Jeffrey were dodging behind cabins on their way back from the woods. They were off to meet the guys at the lean-to in blue territory, because it was just about halfway through game time.

Mike was wearing a watch today, so he knew the horn would be sounding soon. He thought they might as well get a head start. He and Jeffrey had just passed the cabins near the lake when they heard a commotion.

"Get him! Stop that dog! Anyone!" the red guards called. But no other red players were close enough to hear.

Quickly, Mike and Jeffrey hid behind a cabin.

They watched in awe as Rosco zipped out of the forest from the lake trail, the red flag in his mouth. Their mouths hung open as two red guards appeared from a good distance behind, chasing after him.

The guards and Rosco would be entering the grassy field soon. The orange cone boundary line was just ahead. All Rosco would have to do was cross through the cones from the red side to the blue side, untagged, to win.

"Rosco has the flag!" Jeffrey yelled. "Come on, Mike! Let's stop those girls!"

* * *

James and Caleb had taken the red team kids they'd captured to the blue jail and were returning to the woods to capture more red players.

Caleb squinted. "Look, James! Here comes Rosco! What's he doing?"

James was puzzled. "That's weird. I thought Mandy said Rosco was going with her today. I don't see the girls anywhere." He squinted too, scanning the trail behind Rosco.

Soon, Rosco shot by, racing toward the field, but still too far away for James and Caleb to see exactly what was happening.

Next, the red team girls who'd been chasing Rosco appeared, captured by Mike and Jeffrey. The girls were walking slowly, short of breath from their long run through the woods. Mike and Jeffrey held them by the elbows.

James and Caleb caught up to them quickly.

"Guys, Rosco's got the flag!" Jeffrey said.

CHAPTER 20

YOU CAN
DO IT, BOY

James and Caleb quickly followed Mike, Jeffrey and the captured red team guards to the field. Other red team campers swarmed to tag the speedy dog. He was on their side of the field, and he had to cross the cones to get to safety on the blue side.

"Go, Rosco! You can do it, boy!" James shouted.

Rosco raced in circles around the field. This was just like keep-away, only better! No one could tag him. He was just too fast.

"Come on, Sheriff! Help the red team catch him!" a counselor called. "Only another dog can catch Rosco! He's too fast for two-legged creatures!"

Sheriff had been lying quietly in the shade. It was much hotter this afternoon than it had been last night during the game before the rain. So he'd been happy to stay right where he was, hoping to sit this one out. He was watching with amusement as his fellow red team members defended the boundary line, when the counselors called to him.

Okay, he might as well give them what they wanted. He huffed and shook himself. If nothing else, he might be able to corner Rosco, so one of the kids could tag him. Sheriff figured that ought to let him off the hook.

Mandy, Kimberly, and Margaret arrived at the field with their captor.

"Look!" Mandy cried. "He made it all the way here! Rosco made it!"

The guard who had Mandy's arm tossed her ponytail proudly. "Yeah, but he'll never get past all of our defenders," she said. Mandy noticed she looked worried, watching the activity on the field.

Three red team players were coming at Rosco from behind, and two red team players were coming at him from ahead. But Rosco darted away easily.

Sheriff thought about how he didn't *really* want to ruin the fun for Rosco. After all, Rosco's impressive energy and wits had helped him take the flag this far. Rosco had come a long way and earned this near-victory. Sheriff hated to take it away from Rosco. After all, he had just finally come around to liking the youngster.

But Sheriff couldn't let his team down. He would play by the rules, no matter what. He would play fair. He would try his best to help, so that the kids could tag Rosco.

So Sheriff hauled himself to his feet, ran over, and stood firmly in front of Rosco. When Rosco pounced a little to the left, Sheriff quickly pounced to the left. When Rosco pounced to the right, Sheriff pounced to the right. Rosco couldn't get around him.

Soon, the red team kids and Sheriff had cornered him. Rosco had to think fast.

He'd charm the old dog and make a run for it. There was no time to waste. Out of the blue, he flashed a great big doggy smile at Sheriff. Sheriff relaxed for just a moment, letting down his guard and returning a genuine smile.

This is it! Rosco thought. This is my chance!

Before anyone could stop him, Rosco bolted between the bulky bullmastiff and the oncoming kids. He raced toward the boundary line. In a few seconds he crossed between two orange cones and safely reached the blue side.

A roar of excitement rose from the blue team. "He did it!"

Blue team players looked at each other in disbelief. "We won! We captured their flag! Rosco did it!"

Tony blew the horn to signify that the game had ended.

James and the rest of the blue team rushed over to Rosco. Mandy broke free from her stunned captor and raced to Rosco's side.

James took the flag from Rosco's mouth and patted him heartily on the back. He held the flag high in the air as his teammates cheered.

"Good boy, Rosco! Good boy! You did it!" he said. Rosco danced about with excitement.

James, Caleb, Mike, and Jeffrey high fived each other. Everyone had played fairly and looked out for one another. Josh, Tim, and Jeremiah waved their fists in the air and chanted, "Go, blue! Go, blue!" Mandy, Kim, and Margaret jumped up and down with excitement.

Tony grabbed his megaphone. "This is the first time in Camp Hickory Ridge history that a dog has ever brought home the flag to win the game! Let's hear it for Rosco!"

The blue team cheered. The red team smiled, despite themselves, and clapped along. They had tried their best. And no one could argue with the fact that the teams were fair. A dog had been placed on each team, after all. No one had said that the dogs couldn't actually *play* the game.

But Rosco, even though he was thrilled with their victory, wondered if Sheriff would be upset with him all over again. Rosco might have tricked Sheriff with his rascally grin out on the field, but he sure hoped Sheriff didn't mind, because Rosco really wanted to be pals.

Sheriff trotted over. Rosco stopped panting and peered at him, looking for an answer. The big, old dog winked proudly at him and barked softly. *You got me, kid. You tricked me with that goofy grin! But you earned this, and I'm glad. Good job.*

On another part of the field, Mandy ran to tell James how she had been the one to find the flag. Wide-eyed, James slapped hands with his sister proudly.

"Wow! That's incredible, Mandy," he said. "You're a natural at this game. And hey, I bet you really understand what I meant about camp now, don't you? That you'd love it here once you gave it a chance?"

"I sure do, James. I wish I could stay here all summer now," Mandy said. "This place is the best. I already can't wait to come back next year!" She realized with satisfaction that she hadn't been homesick in days.

About The Author

Shana Gorian, originally from western Pennsylvania, lives in Southern California with her husband, two children, and her German shepherd, the real *Rosco*. Shana spent many memorable summers at sleep-away camp as a child, and later, as a camp counselor. She loves to talk and write about the virtues of summer camp!

Ros Webb is an artist based in Ireland. She has produced a multitude of work for books, digital books and websites. Samples of her art can be seen on Facebook: Ros Webb Book Illustration.

Josh Addessi is a quirky illustrator and animation professor based in Northwest Indiana. He has digitally painted all manner of book covers, stage backdrops and trading cards. Samples of his art can be seen at http://joshaddessi.blogspot.com/

Tori March is an illustrator and 3D sculptor. She aided in painting the forest and camp for this book cover. Samples of her art can be seen at https://www.artstation.com/artist/victoriamarch

The *real* Rosco is every bit as loveable and rascally as the fictional Rosco. He loves to capture flags, too.

Visit **shanagorian.com** to keep up with Rosco and his upcoming adventures. And be sure to join him for more adventures in the other books in the series!

Made in the USA
Middletown, DE
08 August 2021